Contents

ADAM★SHARP
• Moose Master •

by George Edward Stanley
illustrated by Guy Francis

SCHOLASTIC INC.
New York   Toronto   London   Auckland   Sydney
Mexico City   New Delhi   Hong Kong   Buenos Aires

To Andy and Karen and Al and Gail—
thanks for all the Michigan memories!
—G.E.S.

To Bill and Bob
—G.F.

ISBN 0-439-68355-6

12 11 10 9 8 7 6 5 4 3 2 1   5 6 7 8 9 10/0

Printed in the U.S.A   08

First Scholastic printing, February 2005

1
Showoff

"Om," Adam Sharp said. He was meditating.

Life as an eight-year-old super spy for IM-8 could be stressful. Yoga helped him to relax.

"Om," Adam said again.

He opened one eye. He checked the clock. "Yay!" he shouted. He had ten minutes before his bedtime. It was time to play.

Adam sat down next to his new wooden

toy logs and worked on his model of the CIA building. Adam had been inside it many times. Sometimes the CIA and IM-8 worked together on cases.

Adam liked his new wooden logs. They were made in Canada by the Ecanem Lumber Company.

Just then, Adam's secret telephone rang. The only person who had the number was T. T was the head of IM-8.

Adam picked up the phone. "Sharp here!" he said.

"Meet me at the airport right away!" T said. "You have another mission!"

"Yes, sir!" Adam said. He took off his

pajamas and put on his tuxedo. He raced downstairs. His parents were watching TV.

"My teacher called," Adam said. "I'm going on a Gifted and Talented field trip."

There wasn't really a Gifted and Talented Program at Friendly Elementary School. It was a cover for IM-8.

"A field trip! What fun!" his mother said.

"We're very proud of you, Adam," his father told him. "You are such a good student. Even late at night!"

"I try," Adam said modestly.

T was waiting for Adam at the airport. J was with him. J was the janitor at Friendly Elementary School. He also made IM-8's secret gadgets.

"The Royal Canadian Mounted Police need IM-8's help. You're going to Canada," T told Adam. "For the next few days, you'll be a Mountie!"

"Hurray!" Adam shouted. Then he blushed. Spies should never act excited about things. "I mean, I'm all ready, sir."

The Mounties were a police force in Canada. Adam liked their horses and their hats. He *really* liked the hats.

J handed Adam a can of peas. "Don't forget your gear," J said. "It has everything you need for camping out."

"Thanks, J," Adam said. He put the can in his pocket and turned to T. "Who's our contact with the Mounties?" he asked.

"Mabel Leaf," T said.

"Mabel Leaf," Adam said. "I'll radio her from the IM-8 jet."

"We're not taking the IM-8 jet, Sharp," T said. He led Adam down the runway. "We're taking the IM-8 pontoon plane."

"The pontoon plane?" Adam didn't even know IM-8 *had* a pontoon plane!

In minutes, they were in the air and headed to Canada. Adam took a power nap while they flew over Ontario. He woke up when they reached the north woods.

The pontoon plane landed on the river. Mabel Leaf was standing on the bank. She had on her Royal Canadian Mounted Police uniform. Her jacket was bright red. Her boots were shiny. She was holding the reins of two horses.

Adam jumped out of the plane and waded to shore. He wished he had shiny boots. Adam didn't like getting his feet wet.

"Welcome to Canada, Yank!" Mabel said.

Adam smiled. "Yank" was what some Canadians called Americans. "Thanks," he said. "What's the problem, Mabel?"

"I'll tell you on the way to base camp," Mabel said. "It's twenty kilometers east of here."

Kilometers? Of course! The metric system. Canada used kilometers instead of miles. Luckily, Adam knew the metric system as perfectly as he knew French, German, and Greek.

"It's a long ride, Yank," Mabel said, "so mount up!"

Adam patted his horse's nose. "What's her name?" he asked.

"Showoff!" Mabel said.

"*Showoff?*" Adam said. "Why?"

"You'll see," Mabel said.

2
Night Mission

Showoff took off. Adam held on tight.
Showoff was fast. The wind felt like a
hurricane in Adam's face.

Showoff jumped over rocks and fallen
logs. Showoff ran circles around the trees.
Showoff balanced with two hooves on the
side of a cliff.

In other words, Showoff showed off.

Finally, Showoff slowed down. Adam

caught his breath while Mabel filled him in. The problem had to do with lumber.

"You see, Yank, logrolling contests are how the government of Canada decides who gets to cut down the trees," Mabel said. "And one company always wins the logrolling contests. Ecanem."

Adam gave her a funny look. *"Ecanem?* They make great toy logs! I play with mine all the time," he said. "What's the problem?"

Mabel sighed. "Ecanem is putting the other lumber companies out of business."

"How awful!" Adam said. He began to say something else. But then he had a weird feeling. Like they were being watched!

Adam looked over his shoulder. No one was there. Just bunnies and squirrels and a herd of moose. Adam shook off the feeling.

A few minutes later, Adam and Mabel came to a river. They rode their horses into the water. Adam pulled his feet up.

Out of the corner of his eye, Adam saw something upstream. Several logs suddenly popped up in the river.

"Mabel," Adam said, "those logs came out of nowhere!"

"That's impossible, Yank!" Mabel said.

The logs were headed right toward them. They seemed to be moving faster than the water.

"Hurry!" Mabel shouted. "They're going to hit us!" She spurred her horse.

But Showoff stayed where she was.

"Giddy-up, Showoff!" Adam shouted.

The logs were closing in.

Finally, Showoff made her move.

She jumped over the first log. She jumped over the second log. She jumped over all the logs until she and Adam reached the other side of the river.

"Showoff should join the circus!" Adam said.

Mabel grinned. "That's where she was before the Mounties."

Adam was surprised to see the herd of

moose cross the river, too. *That's odd,* he thought. *They seem to be following us!*

Adam and Mabel rode deeper into the woods. "We have to go around the Ecanem Sawmill," Mabel said. "Base camp is on the other side."

"Hey! Let's stop and take a tour!" Adam said. "Maybe they'll give us free toy logs."

"Sorry, Yank," Mabel said. "It's just not

that kind of place. Here, I'll show you."

They rode to the top of a hill. In the valley below, the Ecanem Sawmill was surrounded by tall fences and guard towers.

"It looks like a prison," Adam said. "Not a friendly toy-making company!"

Suddenly, a loud siren went off.

"Quick! We have to get out of here!" Mabel said. "If they see us, I'll be in trouble. Mounties aren't supposed to spy on people."

They turned the horses and rode to Mountie base. All the Mounties came out to greet Adam. He shook their hands.

"I need to look and act just like a Mountie," Adam said. "Show me how."

One Mountie helped Adam put on a uniform. Another Mountie helped Adam put on a hat. A third Mountie gave Adam a mirror. Adam liked what he saw.

When Adam was ready, the Mounties had a Mountie meeting.

"We think Ecanem is cheating at the logrolling contests," Mabel said. "But we can't prove it. There's another contest next week. We need an agent there. Someone Ecanem doesn't know."

"I'll do it!" Adam said.

"Hurray!" the Mounties cheered.

"Do you know how to roll logs?" Mabel asked.

"No," Adam said. "But I'm a fast learner. I learned to skydive in two hours."

"Wow!" the Mounties said.

"All I need is a good teacher," Adam said. "Who is the best logroller?"

Mabel stepped out of line. "That's me!"

Adam noticed the other Mounties had funny looks on their faces.

"Then let's get started!" Adam said.

Mabel looked up at the sun. "There's not enough time today," she said. "We'll start early in the morning."

I guess the lesson takes longer than I thought, Adam decided. "Okay, I'll just go to my tent," he said.

Mabel turned red. "I'm sorry, Yank. We don't have a guest tent. You have to sleep on the ground."

"No problem," Adam said. "I have my own." He took out the can of peas that J had given him. He pulled the tab on top. Out popped a huge tent. It even had a sign that said MOBILE IM-8 HEADQUARTERS.

"Yank!" Mabel said. "That is so cool!"

"It's just like IM-8 Headquarters—only smaller," Adam said. He put the empty can in his pocket. "Well, good night, Mabel."

"Good night, Yank," Mabel said.

But Adam didn't go to bed. He had a secret mission planned. He needed to take a closer look at the Ecanem Sawmill. Even though Adam was dressed like a Mountie, he was still an IM-8 agent. *And it was his job to spy!*

Adam waited until Mabel and the rest of the Mounties were asleep. Then he saddled Showoff, put on his night-vision goggles, and slipped out of camp.

Ecanem was lit up by searchlights. At night, it looked even more like a prison. With the flick of a switch, the night-vision goggles turned into night-vision binoculars.

Now he could see a big gate opening. Out came men carrying logs over their shoulders. They all had big smiles on their faces.

Why are these men so happy? Adam wondered. *And where are they taking those logs?*

3

The Secret Training Camp

The next morning, Adam followed Mabel to a big pond full of logs. The herd of moose was grazing nearby. Now a short, ugly moose had joined them.

Adam didn't say anything to Mabel about his secret mission. He didn't want to get her in trouble.

"Everyone brings his or her own log to the contest, Yank," Mabel said. "So pick the one you like best." She jumped onto a log. She started rolling it.

"That looks easy," Adam said. He jumped onto a log. He fell off.

"Okay, Sharp! Out of the pond!" Mabel shouted. "This is going to be harder than I thought!"

Adam got out of the pond.

"Normally, all Mounties go through a tough training camp before they start rolling logs," Mabel said. "I just thought that, well, uh . . ."

Adam turned red. "IM-8 training never had logrolling," he told her. "But that will change when I get back to Headquarters!"

Mabel grinned. "Let's start with toe touches!" While Mabel counted to one thousand, Adam touched his toes.

Then he did one thousand sit-ups and jumping jacks. That was followed by one thousand push-ups, stomach crunches, and cartwheels.

Finally, Mabel said, "Try the log again."

Adam looked at his watch. He had been warming up for six hours. It seemed more like six days!

Now Adam knew why the Mounties gave him those funny looks. Mabel was tough!

Adam climbed back on a log.

"Move those feet, Yank!" Mabel shouted. "Roll! Roll! Roll!"

Adam did what Mabel said. But he kept

falling off. No IM-8 training program had ever been this tough. It was also hard to focus with those moose around.

Am I crazy? Adam wondered. *Or is that short, ugly moose laughing every time I fall?*

Adam kept trying to roll the log. Just when he thought he was getting better, he'd fall off again. And the short, ugly moose would snicker.

But Adam wasn't going to let a moose make him nervous. A lot of people in Canada were counting on him.

Finally, Adam had the hang of it. "We can practice more tomorrow," he said.

At dawn, Adam heard the moose outside. But by the time he had put on his uniform and his hat and looked at himself in the mirror, the moose were gone.

Mabel was just coming out of her tent.

"I think the moose are up to no good!" Adam said. "Let's follow them."

Mabel raised an eyebrow. "What about logrolling practice?" she said.

"It'll have to wait," Adam said. He was sure Mabel thought he was trying to get out of training. But that didn't matter. IM-8 agents always had to put their spying first!

Adam and Mabel got on their horses. They headed across the meadow toward the woods.

When they reached the trees, Mabel pointed
to the ground. "Tracks!" she said. She and
Adam jumped off their horses.

"These are from a huge wolf. These are
from a huge bear. These are from a huge
mountain lion," Mabel told him.

"Which ones are from the moose?"
Adam asked.

Mabel pointed to several hoof tracks.

"That's strange," Adam said. "Some of the tracks don't look like hooves. They look like they were made by tennis shoes!"

Mabel looked closely. "You're right! But why would a moose wear tennis shoes?"

Adam and Mabel got back on their horses and rode deeper into the woods. From time to time, they stopped to study the tracks.

"Most of the herd left here," Mabel said.

"But the moose with the tennis shoes went deeper into the woods," Adam said. "We need to follow it!"

The trees were so thick that Adam could

hardly see the path in front of him.

Mabel stopped her horse. She put a hand to her ear. She listened. "Yank!" she gasped. "I hear people singing the National Lumberjack Song!"

They got off their horses. They crawled slowly on their bellies toward the voices.

The singing got louder and louder. They came to an opening in the trees. Before them, they saw a huge pond. Several lumberjacks were rolling logs in the water.

Adam knew the lumberjacks right away. He had seen them leaving the sawmill last night! "It's a secret lumberjack training camp!" Adam whispered.

Adam couldn't believe how fast they were logrolling. They never fell off, either.

For a moment, Adam was jealous. *Will I ever be that good?* he wondered.

Adam shook off his doubt. It was not worthy of an IM-8 agent.

"Look, Adam," Mabel said.

Adam looked. In the middle of the pond was a huge pile of sticks and branches. "A beaver lodge!" He looked more closely. "Is that the short, ugly moose sitting on top of it?"

"Yes!" Mabel said. "Why in the world is it sitting on a beaver lodge?"

4

General Ecanem

Adam and Mabel circled the pond. Now that he was closer, Adam could see each lumberjack had something in his hands. It looked like a TV remote control.

From time to time, the lumberjacks aimed the controls at their logs and pushed a button. The logs turned fast. The logs turned slowly.

Adam remembered the logs that had

popped up in the river on their way to Mountie base.

"They have remote-control logs!" Adam whispered to Mabel.

Adam and Mabel sneaked closer.

Just then, the short, ugly moose stood on his hind legs. He put his front hooves up to his face, and then—he pulled off his head!

Adam gasped.

"Adam! That's not a short, ugly moose in tennis shoes!" Mabel said. "That's General Ecanem in a moose costume! He owns the Ecanem Lumber Company!"

"I know him by another name, Mabel. General *Menace*! He's my archenemy!" Adam said. He slammed his fist into his hand. "Of course! *Ecanem is Menace spelled backward!* This beaver lodge must be General Menace's new headquarters!"

"How evil!" Mabel said. "I bet he's trying to take over the world's lumber market. We need to warn the Mounties!"

Adam and Mabel raced back to the horses. But the way was blocked. The herd of moose had cut them off. They were trapped!

"Mabel, these moose work for General Menace!" Adam said.

Suddenly, the moose opened their mouths. They made loud moose calls.

Adam knew they were warning General
Menace.

He and Mabel were doomed.

These moose weren't going to let them
go anywhere!

5

The Logrolling Champ

Adam had an idea. He looked straight at the moose. "Heh! Heh! Heh!" he said.

The moose all blinked in surprise. They stopped making moose calls.

Just as Adam had planned, the moose thought it was General Menace's evil laugh! They weren't sure if Adam and Mabel were friends or enemies.

"Walk toward the horses," Adam

whispered to Mabel. "Heh! Heh! Heh!" he said again to the moose.

"HEY! That's Adam Sharp and Mabel Leaf!" General Menace shouted. "DON'T LET THEM ESCAPE!"

"HEH! HEH! HEH!" Adam shouted.

The moose were confused. General Menace was shouting orders at them. Adam was heh-heh-hch-ing at them.

Adam and Mabel had reached the edge of the clearing.

General Menace and the lumberjacks rolled their logs across the pond as fast as they could. Soon they'd be at the bank.

"Let's get out of here!" Adam cried.

He and Mabel untied their horses and jumped on. They raced through the woods. The tree branches whipped at their faces.

They came to a river. It was full of logs!

Adam spotted a large crowd on the other bank. He wondered if people in Canada watched floating logs for fun.

"The horses have to jump the logs!" Mabel said.

Adam wasn't worried. Showoff knew how to show off. But Showoff wouldn't budge. Neither would Mabel's horse.

Adam could hear General Menace and his lumberjacks in the woods. They were almost to the river!

"We can't wait here, Mabel!" he yelled. "We need to roll the logs ourselves!" He jumped off his horse.

"Do you think you're ready?" Mabel asked.

"IM-8 agents are always ready!" Adam told her bravely. He hoped this time it was true.

Adam and Mabel jumped onto the first log. They rolled. They jumped onto the second one. They rolled some more.

Behind them, General Menace and his lumberjacks had reached the riverbank. They jumped onto the logs, too.

Adam looked over his shoulder. The lumberjacks could hardly stand up. They could barely roll a log.

How did they ever win a contest? Adam wondered.

"Mabel!" Adam shouted. "They bring the remote-control logs to the contests! That's why they win!"

"You're right!" Mabel shouted back. "But the remote controls don't work on these logs!"

Adam focused on his logrolling. He tried

to become one with the log. It was all in the timing.

Once or twice he almost fell. But Mabel was a good teacher. She had given him some great tips.

He and Mabel rolled the logs across the water. Adam heard splashes behind him. It was the lumberjacks falling into the river.

Adam and Mabel reached the other side. The crowd went wild. A bunch of Mounties ran toward them.

"You won!" the Mounties cried. "You beat Ecanem's lumberjacks!"

Adam was shocked. "But the logrolling contest isn't until next week," he said.

"The Canadian government changed the time," a Mountie said. "They decided a surprise contest would be more fair."

Adam turned. General Menace was wading toward the bank. Water poured off his uniform. A little fish flopped out of his

pocket. He waved his fist at Adam. "You won't get away from me this time, Sharp!" He signaled to his moose.

Just then, the IM-8 pontoon plane landed on the river. It made a huge wave that knocked over General Menace. He started floating down the river.

"Hurry, Sharp!" T called from the plane. "You're needed for another mission!"

"How did T know where you were?" Mabel asked.

Adam pulled the empty can of peas out of his pocket. "The can is a satellite dish," he said.

"IM-8 is amazing," Mabel said. "You

saved all of the lumber companies from
going out of business."

"Thanks, Mabel," Adam said. He shook
hands with her. "It was great being a
Mountie." Adam took off his hat, looked at
it, and sighed.

"Keep the hat, Adam," Mabel said. "You
earned it."

"Do you mean it?" Adam asked. He *really*
liked the hat.

"Yes, Yank," Mabel said. "You may be
IM-8's best spy. But you'll always be a
Mountie to me!"